THE BATTLE OF SILLYVILLE

LIVE SILLY OR DIE!

by Peter Hannan

Alfred A. Knopf, Publisher New York

THIS IS A BORZOI BOOK PUBLISHED BY ALFRED A. KNOPF, INC.

Copyright © 1991 by Peter Hannan
All rights reserved under International and Pan-American Copyright
Conventions. Published in the United States by Alfred A. Knopf, Inc.,
New York, and simultaneously in Canada by Random House of Canada
Limited, Toronto. Distributed by Random House, Inc., New York.

Library of Congress Cataloging-in-Publication Data
Hannan, Peter.
  The battle of Sillyville / by Peter Hannan.
     p.   cm.
  Summary: Lemuel B. Nutty comes to the aid of the residents of
Sillyville when Delbert S. Dullard threatens to turn the town into
Drabville II.
     ISBN 0-679-80286-X (pbk.)—ISBN 0-679-90286-4 (lib. bdg.)
     [1. Humorous stories.]   I. Title.
PZ7.H1978Bat   1991
[E]—dc20   90-4544   CIP   AC

Manufactured in the United States of America
10 9 8 7 6 5 4 3 2 1

This book is dedicated to my son, Cole,
whose story about turning into a toaster
served as a major inspiration.

In the middle of a pleasant dream, in the middle of the night, I was rudely awakened by a loud pounding on my window.

In climbed a very nervous character who was talking a million miles a minute.

I knew a hardened criminal when I saw one. I hurled myself at the intruder with all my might, and as we crashed to the floor I picked out one familiar word from his endless chatter: *Sillyville.*

Sillyville was a secret town full of very strange people that my sister Ruby and I knew and loved. "What did you say?" I asked.

He took a deep breath and spoke more slowly. "My name is Iguana Monkeywrench, and I've got a message from the people of Sillyville."

Ruby and I couldn't wait to hear news about our favorite place on earth. "How's that nutty mayor? Are things as silly as ever?"

Iguana Monkeywrench looked glum. "Things are not good. The goons from the neighboring town of Drabville have invaded! They have some documents that prove the old boundaries between the two towns were drawn incorrectly. Sillyville isn't even on their new maps. They're calling it Drabville II."

"We're so sorry," said Ruby.

Iguana begged, "You must come help us. PLEASE!"

"We'd love to help," I said, "but our mom and dad would definitely not approve."

"Then again," said Ruby, "I suppose we could leave a note. That should put their minds at ease...."

On the way, we heard more terrible details of the Sillyville situation.

Iguana Monkeywrench was driving very fast, but it seemed like it took days to get there.

When we finally arrived, we didn't recognize the place. The residents were sleepwalking.

Everywhere we looked, Drabville goons were standing around acting goony. In the town square a statue of Sillyville's beloved founding

father was being replaced by a statue of the self-proclaimed emperor of Drabville II.

Iguana led us to the mayor's house, where an emergency meeting had been called.
Residents spoke their minds.

All eyes turned to Ruby and me. "Please advise us. What can we do?" they asked.

We were stumped.

When I finally opened my mouth, I hated the words that spilled out.

Jeez, maybe you could just learn... uh, to live with boredom?

Suddenly a little old man stumbled over the mayor's dog and into the room.

We could hardly believe our eyes. Falling before us was Lemuel B. Nutty, the founder of Sillyville himself.

"But where have you been all these years?" somebody asked.

Oh, I did a little traveling by whaleback, learned to juggle jelly, surfed the lava flow of the Mooka Mooka Volcano, I was married to a purty little lady from Mars for a spell, I roomed with grizzlies for a few decades, I ran a ski resort in Mexico City, taught poetry to flies and mosquitos.

After a while he got around to the problem at hand. "You youngsters arrange for me a one-on-one duel with that no-good Delbert S. Dullard and we'll send those Drabvillians packing."

We wondered if his age might be a problem.

But Mr. Nutty, you are, well, rather... mature, and that Dullard is as big and strong as an ox!

But Mr. Nutty would have none of it.

And ten times as dumb as an ox! This will be a battle of wits, my silly friend.

With no other options on the table, in desperation we decided to go ahead with the duel. It was easy to get the goons to agree to it. We offered a cash prize.

And Delbert S. Dullard loved money even more than he loved boredom.

The duel was held the next day. Supporters on both sides were there in great number.

The duelists entered the ring. Dullard was even bigger than I had imagined.

Ruby and I couldn't bear to look. We were sure Lemuel B. Nutty was done for.

But then he started talking.

"Oh, yes, I'm quite sure you'll have no problem with a withered senior citizen such as myself, but since these fine folks have come to see a show, I'm sure you wouldn't mind first playing a quick round of 'Riddle, Riddle, Who's Got the Riddle,' unless, of course, you're CHICKEN…?"

"CHICKEN?! I'll beat you at anything, old man!"
Delbert replied. And he started right in.

The crowd burst into laughter.

"And why is a Drabvillian like an all-corn-on-the-cob meal?"

"Wha—?"

"Nothing between the ears!"

The crowd went wild.

"What do Drabvillians read each morning?" Lemuel continued.

"Huh?"

"The snooze paper."

Lemuel B. Nutty asked riddles while standing on his head. He asked riddles while standing on Delbert S. Dullard's head.

He hammered away at the big oaf with riddle after riddle, until Dullard's face turned as red as a fire truck. Smoke poured out of his ears and he was blind with rage.

"Okay," said Delbert S. Dullard, "enough of this nonsense. It's time to *fight*."

Dizzy, confused, and unable even to find his opponent, Dullard began punching wildly at the air.

Lemuel B. Nutty leaped gracefully toward him. He placed his index finger on Dullard's forehead and gently pushed him over.

Delbert S. Dullard landed with a thud.

A hush came over the crowd.

Dullard looked up at Lemuel B. Nutty. "I forged those documents. Sillyville is yours. It was always yours. It will be yours forever. I'm happy to be rid of this idiotic little Podunk town."

Lemuel B. Nutty was declared Exalted Royal
Silliness of the Universe, and a celebration began.

And when the Sillyville Off-Key Choir started
singing the town song, everyone joined in:

"Oh, Sillyville, oh, Sillyville,
   You crazy little city,
No one can ever make you change,
   Not even one small bitty.
Your loony laws just make no sense,
   Your landlords don't charge any rents.
Oh, Sillyville, oh, Sillyville,
   You crazy little city."